Issun B

or One-Inch Boy

retold by Lori O'Dea

illustrated by Coco Masuda

Make Inferences

Look at the characters from this story. What can you tell about them?

An old man and woman
saw children.
They saw big and small children.
They saw boys and girls.

They made a wish.
"We want a child, any child!"
Soon they had a little boy.
They called him Issun Boshi,
or One-Inch Boy.

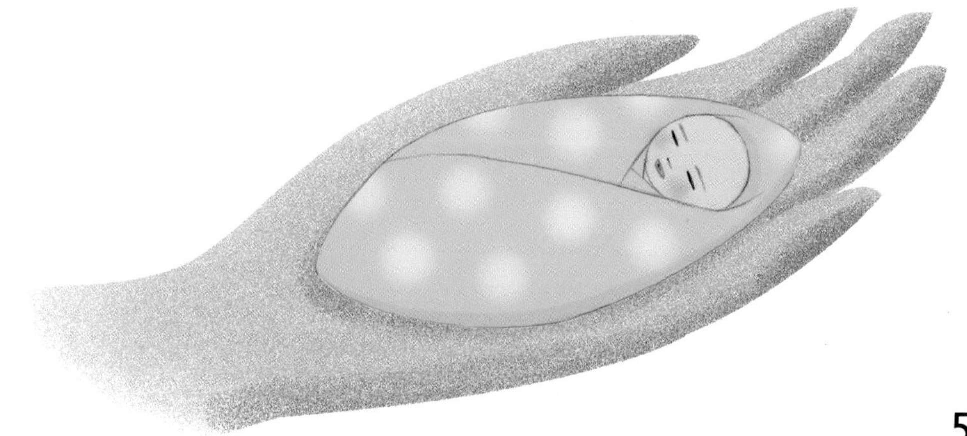

Issun Boshi was a good boy.
He was not big, but he was brave.

He wanted to go many places.
He went away in a rice bowl.
He had a pin for a sword.

He got to the city.
He saw a big house.
"I want to work!" he said.

The princess liked him.
“I will work for you,” he said.

One day they went out.
They saw a bad giant.

The princess was afraid.

Issun Boshi ran up the giant's arm.

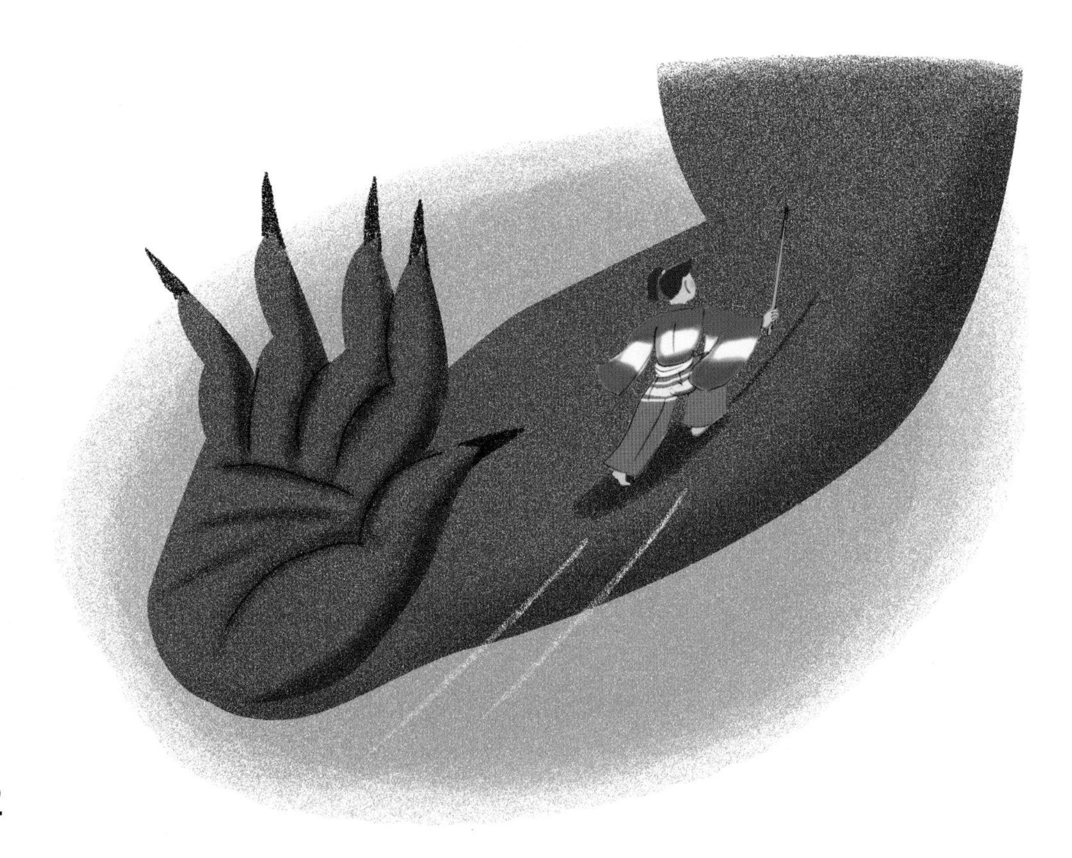

"OUCH!" cried the giant.

Issun Boshi ran back down the giant's arm.

The giant ran away.

"Thank you, Issun Boshi,"
the princess said.
She closed her eyes and made
a wish.

She opened her eyes.
Issun Boshi was tall!
Everyone was very happy!